This book belongs to

. . . .

For Ava
With love from Mummy.

EGMONT
We bring stories to life

Lydia Monks

Go, Go, Gorilla!

EGMONT

Hurrah! My friend had arrived at last!
He had come to stay with me for a few days.
I was excited, and he was excited too.

"Ooo, ooo, OOO!"
I think he was going to like it.

We'd bought lots of food we thought he would like,
and cooked a meal especially for him.

We had banana broth,

followed by
banana burgers,

with banoffee pie
for dessert.

"Ooo, ooo, ooo!"
he said.
I think he liked it.

When we went to bed, I let him have
the top bunk. I thought
he'd feel more at home there.

"Ooo, ooo, OOO!"
he said as he snuggled up for the night.
I think he liked it.

Overnight it had snowed.
He had never seen snow before.

He licked it,

poked it,

tasted it,

and sat in it,
before he said,
"Ooo, ooo, ooo!"

I think he liked it.

We thought we would take him out
for the day and do lots of snowy things.

First we took him skiing.
We thought he'd like that.

But he wibbled

and wobbled

and wiggled

all over the place,

until he toppled over

and rolled all the way

down the ski slope.

"Ooo, ooo, ooo, ooo!" he moaned.

I don't think he liked it.

So we took him skating.
We thought he would like that.

But he wibbled

and wobbled

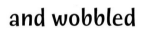

and wiggled
all over the place
until . . .

... he slipped and fell with a big bump on his **big bottom.**

"Ooo, ooo, ooo!" he groaned.

I don't think he liked it.

By this time, Gorilla was feeling very sorry for himself,
so we took him off to make snowmen.

We thought he'd like that.

But his snowman wibbled

and wobbled
and wiggled
all over the place until . . .

. . . it fell right on top of him!
"Ooo, **OOO, OOO!**" he cried.

He **didn't** like it.

I wondered how to make him feel better.
Then I thought of something . . .

"There must be lots of things you *are* good at," I said.
"I bet you're good at swinging!"

With that, Gorilla smiled.
He lifted me up onto
his back and started
to climb the nearest tree.

Then he swung . . .

But we didn't fall.

And our Ooo, ooo, ooos turned into
Hoo, hoo, hoos! and Ha, ha, hahs!
He was laughing, and I was laughing, too.

He DID like it!

Gorilla felt so much better.
He decided to have just
one more try at skiing,
and skating, and
making a snowman.

And although he still wibbled
and wobbled and wiggled,
he just kept on laughing.

"Ooo, ooo, ooo,
Hoo, hoo, hoo,
Ha, ha, ha!"

And I kept on laughing too.

I was a bit sad when it was time
for Gorilla to go home,

but I *knew* we would be seeing him again soon.

Next time it would be our turn to visit and . . .

...Ooo, Ooo, OOO!

I knew I was going to like it!